LOOK FOR ALL OF OMAR'S ADVENTURES

PLANET OMAR: Accidental Trouble Magnet

PLANET OMAR: Unexpected Super Spy

PLANET OMAR: Incredible Rescue Mission

PLANET OMAR: Epic Hero Flop

PLANET OMAR
ACCIDENTAL TROUBLE MAGNET

ZANIB MIAN

ILLUSTRATED BY
NASAYA MAFARIDIK

G. P. PUTNAM'S SONS

G. P. PUTNAM'S SONS
An imprint of Penguin Random House LLC, New York

First published in the United States of America by G. P. Putnam's Sons,
an imprint of Penguin Random House LLC, 2019
First paperback edition published 2022

Text copyright © 2019 by Zanib Mian
Illustrations copyright © 2019 by Nasaya Mafaridik
First published in Great Britain by Hodder and Stoughton, 2019
First American edition, 2019

Excerpt from *Planet Omar: Unexpected Super Spy* text copyright © 2020 by Zanib Mian,
illustrations copyright © 2020 by Nasaya Mafaridik
Published by arrangement with Hodder and Stoughton Limited
First published in the United Kingdom in 2020 | First American edition, 2020

Visit us online at penguinrandomhouse.com

THE LIBRARY OF CONGRESS HAS CATALOGED THE HARDCOVER EDITION AS FOLLOWS:
Names: Mian, Zanib, author. | Mafaridik, Nasaya, illustrator.
Title: Accidental trouble magnet / Zanib Mian; illustrated by Nasaya Mafaridik.
Description: First American edition. | New York: G. P. Putnam's Sons, 2020. |
Series: Planet Omar | "First published in Great Britain by Hodder and Stoughton, 2019." |
Summary: "Imaginative Omar goes through the ups and downs of starting a new school and
making new friends with the help of his wonderful (and silly) Muslim family"
—Provided by publisher.
Identifiers: LCCN 2019047166 (print) | LCCN 2019047167 (ebook) | ISBN 9780593109212 |
ISBN 9780593109229 (ebook)
Subjects: CYAC: Family life—England—Fiction. | Muslims—Fiction. | Schools—Fiction. |
Friendship—Fiction. | England—Fiction. | Humorous stories.
Classification: LCC PZ7.1.M514 Acc 2020 (print) | LCC PZ7.1.M514 (ebook) | DDC [Fic]—dc23
LC record available at https://lccn.loc.gov/2019047166
LC ebook record available at https://lccn.loc.gov/2019047167

Printed in the United States of America
ISBN 9780593109236

4th Printing

LSCH

Design by Dave Kopka and Suki Boynton
Text set in Averia Serif Libre

This book is dedicated to all

the children who ever felt that

being different is a negative thing.

ME

my name is Omar
— this is my face

I have a
(HUGE)
imagination

I hate
carrots
x
x

I once raced against
my dad's car on
my bike — and won!

ESA

Don't be fooled
by this three-year-old's
innocent face

Can scream and cry
louder than an
ambulance siren

Bits of food
can always be found
in his hair

plays with my stuff
and makes it all sticky

I love him but don't tell anyone

MARYAM

Thirteen 13
(but thinks she's sixteen)

× 16

Knows 28 surahs
of the Qur'an
by heart

Was once caught hiding
a stash of peanut
butter cups under
her pillow

Loves to tease me even more
than she loves peanut butter cups

MOM

Doesn't know how to say "no"

A scientist

Hardly ever seen without a cup of coffee in her hands!

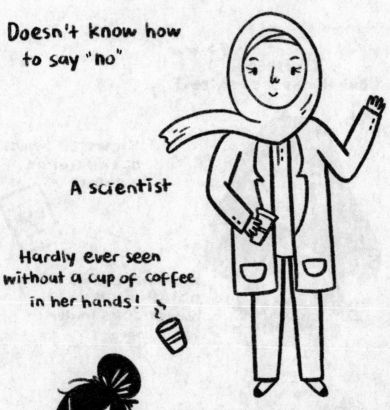

This is what she looks like without her hijab on, when there are no men around who would be allowed to marry her if she didn't already have my dad

DAD

Has a beard because he's copying the greatest man who ever lived — I've never actually seen his face without it

Will never eat a beet

Also a scientist

Has poofy hair
(he says it's because of
   his genes)

Rides a motorcycle
(Grandma tries to
puncture the tires

because she doesn't think
it's safe)

KHAA

CHAPTER 1

TOOoo!

There was a big puddle
of spit on my little
brother's forehead.

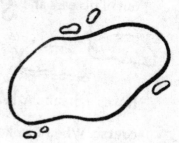

It was mine.

But, **PHEW**, he was still sleeping.

Let me tell you what happened: I had been in my bed, attempting to have a good night's sleep, when suddenly I was being chased through the playground by a teacher who had

GREEN SLIME OOZING

out of his ears and **SLUGS** for fingernails!

It was a dream. A **BAD** dream, of course. When I woke up, I was extremely happy that I wasn't about to be a monster's dinner. I breathed slowly to get my heartbeat back to normal, instead of like it was on a

tRAMPoLiNE.

I remembered that my mom told me to spit toward my shoulder three times if I have a nightmare. That's supposed to get rid of 'SHĀYTĀN', who is the uglyhead who causes bad dreams. I REALLY wanted to get rid of Shaytan! So I conjured up a bucketful of spit in my mouth and SHOT it out over my left shoulder.

THAT'LL TEACH HIM!

I just hoped it would dry before morning so nobody would know I'd spat on my little brother by accident.

I put my head back on the pillow for an eighth of a second, but then I heard a really loud and really annoying sound.

(See? VERY loud and VERY annoying.)

It was Esa. I guess he'd noticed the spit ball after all and wasn't impressed.

Mom appeared at the door to our room in her pajamas, looking all bleary-eyed.

(UNIMPRESSED PARENT
CAN BE RECOGNIZED BY
HAND ON HIP AND
FURROWED EYEBROWS.
CAN BE SCARY, BUT DO
NOT RUN AWAY.)

She said, "What's the matter, Esa?"

Esa was still busy wailing, so I said, "Spit ball."

"Not again, Omar!"

"WAAAAAAAAA!"

I covered my head with the pillow.

Then Dad came in saying that it would be nice

 if we could have

AT LEAST **1** *night*

in the week where

poor Esa isn't woken up by my

SHENANIGANS.

I asked him what that means for the

BILLIONTH time. He rolled his eyes

for the BILLIONTH time.

I heard my big sister, Maryam, growling in

her room. (She definitely doesn't like mornings

very much.)

Mom said it was almost Fajr time anyway.

I wondered if Allah was going to give me a

reward for waking them up for Fajr.

CHAPTER 2

The reason I had been having bad dreams, especially bad dreams about teachers, was because I was going to be starting at a new school. This made me feel like there were

SNAKES in my TUMMY

and some of them were sneaking up and squeezing my heart. I don't like things to change. It would be so much more convenient and better for everybody if things always just stayed the same.

Take my pajamas, for example. They are utterly comfortable pajamas, which have somehow molded their shape to my body and become my second skin. A weird second skin

that I can take off and put on, like some kind of cool human lizard. My mom tried to throw them away and make me wear crispy pajamas that

DON'T EVEN HAVE DINOSAURS ON THEM.

This is change. It's super annoying.

One big, fat, huge change had already happened

to me. We had to move, which is the reason I had

to start at a new school. All this happened because

Mom got her

When she told me, I couldn't help wondering

what she meant exactly by

Did it mean that adults have super-boring

dreams all about jobs? If that was true, I wasn't

looking forward to being an adult, because at the moment I dream about fun stuff, like being on a

ROLLER COASTER that turns into a **flying pig.**

Sometimes, they're even better than movies! Well, apart from the scary ones that make me feel really lucky when I wake up and realize they're not for real.

So, anyway, the job that Mom must have dreamed about all the time was too far from where we lived before, so we had to move.

The moving bit was very, very X 100 ANNOYING

because Dad said I couldn't put all the 1,267 important things from my room in the boxes to take to the new house. He didn't actually count my things, but he likes to say exact numbers when he is talking so he can sound smart. He said I had to choose the ones I love most and give the rest to charity.

Why didn't he understand that

I LOVE THEM ALL?

But then he said he would be very proud of me if I could choose, because I would have done better than Mom, who had already packed lots of what Dad called "boxes of hoarded goods." I like Dad being proud of me (especially because it normally means _pastries_

for breakfast), so I
chose 56 things to take
with me. I counted them really
carefully so I could be precise
when Dad asked (and also make sure
that nobody sneakily gave anything away
without me noticing).

The good news was that the new house
was super, super cool. When we first saw it,
Maryam and I ran straight into the backyard
and whooped, because it was at least twice the
size of our old one. We planned out where
we could put a soccer net
and Esa's swing set,
and Maryam did
loads of cartwheels
to prove just how
massive it was.

WOOO HOOO YAY!

That was the first time we saw the little
old lady who lives next door. She peeped over
her fence and said, "Humph." And she put her
nose higher in the air as if she was smelling
something there that she didn't like.

HUMPH!

CHAPTER 3

School was going to start on Monday. Only two more sleeps before I had to walk into a brand-new classroom with everyone watching and a teacher who might or might not be an

ALIEN ZOMBIE.

Saturday is always mosque day. My mom had decided that for the first few weeks after moving we would visit a different mosque every Saturday and pray Dhuhr there, to see what our new neighborhood was like. Dad normally works on Saturdays, so it was just me, Maryam, Esa and Mom.

My mom is a **VERY SMART SCIENTIST** and works out all sorts of different ways of fighting cancer for the cancer research people. But sometimes Esa's cuteness makes her lose her smartness.

IT'S LIKE HE HAS *big, innocent, smartness-melting eyes.*

They don't work on me, so when Esa wanted to buy a whistle from the gas station on the way to the mosque, I knew it wasn't a good idea. But Mom went right ahead and bought it for him, saying, "Because you've been such a good boy this morning!" and giving him a

on the top of his head. I knew it was gooey because she actually still kisses me like that, even though I've forbidden her to do it in front of my friends.

In the mosque, everyone prays together with the imam leading. It's supposed to be *super quiet*. Just after the prayer began, Esa decided to move from his place. I was praying in between Mom and Maryam. Neither of them moved. I wasn't sure if they'd even noticed that he'd gotten up.

Now, Esa is annoying sometimes, but he IS my little brother, and I worry about him, so I quickly sneaked a look behind us. He was sitting at the back with

A BIG CHEEKY GRIN

on his face. I turned back around and kept on praying. Then we went into Rukhu. That's when your hands are on your knees. Silence from Esa. Then we went into Sujood. That's when your nose and forehead are on the ground.

And then . . .

TWEEEEE!

The loud noise of a whistle broke through the
silence, followed by Esa's voice: "One, two, three,
four, five!" Then again:

And then the counting. It wouldn't stop.

I couldn't help myself. How could I? I

right in the middle of my prayer. I put my

hand over my mouth. I bit my tongue and I even pinched myself really hard, but I couldn't help it! I didn't have to wonder if Mom had heard. People on all floors of the mosque must have heard.

When the prayer finished, Mom and Maryam were a bright shade of pink. It looked as if their skin had suddenly decided to

compete with Maryam's socks for pinkness.

And they were looking everywhere except up at people's faces like they usually do when they greet people after prayers. Mom was motioning angrily to Esa to come to her. Luckily, a few people came and patted Esa's head, which made Mom's skin return to its normal color.

As we were leaving, an old lady with a walking stick and brown abaya waddled over and said:

GOOD COUNTING, YOUNG MAN!

CHAPTER 4

Sunday passed pretty quickly, because Sundays

are science days. Dad calls them

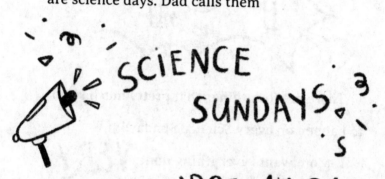

in one of those big **BOOMING**

voices, like it's the most fun you could ever

have on a Sunday. Why? Because my dad is also

a scientist, and I think he and my mom only

had us three kids so that they could create more

scientists or something.

I actually like science, so I don't mind.

We always do fun things, like making slime,

creating fizzy eruptions and making things go

There are four things that pretty much seem to happen on every Science Sunday:

1. Mom wants everything done **VERY** precisely. She's obsessive about it but pretends that she's not, because Science Sundays are supposed to be fun and not bossy. She ends up saying things like, "Just one milliliter more, my sweetheart," through gritted teeth. And, "Are you sure you stirred that correctly, sunshine?"

2. Dad laughs at just how strict Mom gets about the preciseness. And he kisses her head and says that's why she's the best scientist in the world. And she kisses his hand and smiles like she's the luckiest woman in the world

(SUPER YUCK!).

3. Maryam <u>ALWAYS</u> drops important parts of the experiment on the floor.

4. Esa <u>ALWAYS</u> steps on the important parts of the experiment that Maryam drops on the floor. This is because he has **ants in his pants**

and in his shoes and **EVERYWHERE,** and he can't stay still, **EVER.**

That Sunday, we did tornadoes in bottles, which is

SOOO COOL!

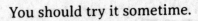

You should try it sometime.

You connect two bottles with a little pipe and you whirl the top bottle, which makes the water go down to the bottom bottle and sends air up, making a tornado.

We all set the things up together, on the kitchen table.

My brain was thinking about telling Maryam to pass the bottles and pipes, but my mouth hadn't caught up with my brain yet and got things muddled up, so it came out as,

Pass the bipes!

Maryam giggled. "Bipes?"

"I mean the bottles and pipes." I giggled, too. "But I like it. BIPES. I wish it was a real word."

"If it was a real word, then it would just be normal and you wouldn't like it anymore," said Maryam.

"That's so true," I said.

Mom and Dad were bending over laughing in the corner of the kitchen. When we asked them what was so funny, they said that in the Arabic language, there's no "p" sound, so a pipe would end up being called a "bibe."

Then Maryam, who was showing off

Googling with her smartphone, said that

actually bipes are a type of

WEIRD DISGUSTING SNAKE-LIZARD

thing that look like they're inside out.

Eventually, we got on with the experiment.

"Oh yeah, tornado in a bottle!" said Dad.

Sometimes he gets really cheesy and excited,

and Maryam and I look at each other and roll

our eyes. (But we kind of like it, really.)

"You can put glitter or food coloring in

the bottle, too, to see the tornado better,"

said Mom, so Maryam and Esa both reached

for the glitter, and Maryam dropped the

bottle on the floor, sending glitter flying
E-V-E-R-Y-W-H-E-R-E.

"Right on schedule," said Dad with a peal of laughter. Mom hugged Maryam and kissed her, also giggling uncontrollably. I could see that Maryam wasn't taking it well.

"URGH!"

She shrugged Mom off and stomped toward the stairs. "Science is so lame anyway."

She does extra-grumpy things like that a lot at the moment. Although it's not like she's ALWAYS grumpy—sometimes she's the nice Maryam, too. It's weird. Dad says it's teenage hormones.

CHAPTER 5

When I woke up on Monday morning, I felt like my lungs were pushing air out of me and not taking any back in, and my stomach was a

GIANT HEAVY ROCK,

making it impossible for me to get out of bed.

REASONS I WAS NERVOUS

what if nobody
likes me?

what if the work
is harder than
at my last school?

$\{ 1/X \, [-10,10,-5,5] \}$

what if nobody
wants to be my
friend?

what if the teacher
is an alien?

Maryam poked her head around the door and said, "Hurry up, *lazyhead*, and stop pretending to be sick."

I wasn't.

I wondered how her lungs felt. She was acting pretty Maryam-like, so her lungs seemed to be normal.

Then Dad appeared at the door, too, and gave her one of his silly looks, which made his face look like he knew a secret. He came in and tickled me and threw me over his right shoulder, then carried me downstairs and plunked me down in front of a bowl of porridge. Now, I know what you might be thinking . . .

YUCK!

But actually, when you put hazelnut spread

into your bowl of porridge, it tastes very

(Though I'm only allowed one spoonful of

the hazelnut spread.)

I ate slowly, because of the rock in my

tummy. Mom said it would be okay and the

teacher would make sure I made friends.

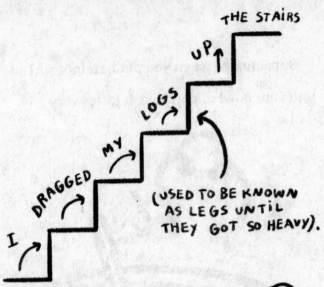

THE STAIRS

UP↑

LOGS

DRAGGED MY

I

(USED TO BE KNOWN AS LEGS UNTIL THEY GOT SO HEAVY).

I washed up and went to my room. There was no uniform at this school, so I was allowed to wear what I wanted.

I looked for my **FAVORITE SWEATSHIRT** and finally pulled it out from the space between my bed and my bedside table. Then I looked for my **FAVORITE JEANS.**

They were exactly where I had left them—
on the floor next to the bookshelf. They
had a stain on them from when Esa threw a
barbecue chicken wing at me. *Oh, well.*
I put them on anyway.

When I went downstairs, my mom went

I mean, she took one look at me and flew
off the handle. She said she couldn't believe
it. That's all she said actually. She said it
five times.

Dad said calmly, "Son, I think Allah has given you clean clothes to wear. So go and put them on, please, or we'll be late."

Then he **H E A V E D** me onto his shoulder again and helped me take out some clothes from my dresser. I put them on

AS FAST AS HUMANLY POSSIBLE

and ran down the stairs. I flew out of the front door toward the car, where Mom was waiting with an angry look on her face.

CHAPTER 6

The thought of
getting into the car
made my tummy feel
like there were

hopping around in it, just waiting to leap up my

throat. So I took a deep breath and imagined a
better way to get to school . . .

ON A SUPER-*Awesome,* *Magnificent* DRAGON!

I could see him there now, just hovering beside
our car and looking at me with a smile. He made
me feel better. About everything. The dragon
bowed his head and flung open the car door for
me, which made me laugh out loud.

"What's so funny, Omar?" Mom asked,
one hand still on the handle of the car door.

But I just shook my head and buttoned
my lips. My mom NEVER really
understands about how I imagine things, so
there was no point explaining—I guess it's
the kind of thing grown-ups forget how
to do.

So I just stared at the dragon's blue and
green shimmery scales and long swooping tail.
As I strapped myself in, I wondered what it
would be like to ride him to school, instead of
driving.

HE'D FLY AT LEAST 120MPH.

He looked at me with his almond-shaped eyes and let out a puff of steam from his tiny nostrils.

I imagined him riding alongside us all the way to school. When we got out and walked to the gate, I made him breathe out a huge plume of steam, and in my head I said,

"I PRONOUNCE THEE H_2O!"

as if I was a **King** or something. I

thought that was a good name for him because

steam is made from water and H_2O is the

chemical name for water (that's the kind of

science-y thing my parents L♡VE to

talk about).

So, there I was. The new kid in

the class. I was petrified and my

lungs were still doing that

funny thing. I made them

feel better by imagining

H_2O being silly at

the window. He

STUCK HIS TONGUE OUT.

Then he put **POPCORN**

in each of his nostrils and blew it out.

The teacher, who was called Mrs. Hutchinson,
introduced me to the class. She was what my
mom would call a pear-shaped person. I liked
her hair from the first time I saw her, and later
learned that the springy auburn curls reacted
to her mood and told the story of her day.
When she was happy, those curls were happy.
They would bounce merrily out of her
head like

When she was tired, they would flop down
lazily on her cheeks. And when she was angry,
they looked more like the twisty metal part
of a drill. Sometimes, when she was angry, I
would imagine a drill-headed Mrs. Hutchinson
making a big hole in the wall quite easily.

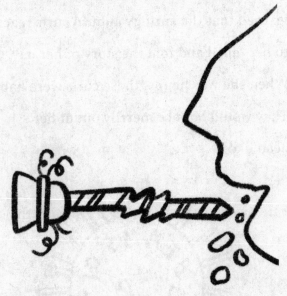

She asked me to sit down next to a
redheaded kid called **Charlie**. Charlie
had lots of freckles all over his face, and

thick-rimmed glasses. I thought he looked cool, so I smiled at him. He smiled back at me. He was missing one of his front teeth.

Charlie told me the school was OK. The lessons were OK. The playground was OK when it wasn't wet. And Mrs. Hutchinson's class was mostly filled with OK kids. Except for Daniel. (I decided that "OK" was Charlie's favorite word.)

"Daniel is the one who you have to look out for, OK? Just stay out of his way."

"OK," I said.

I thought about all the times my mom had told me to stay away from something, which seemed to make me drawn toward it like a

MAGNET

instead. Like when **I JUST HAD TO** open Maryam's secret box, because I was told I wasn't allowed to, and when I did, a gazillion teeny, tiny beads came pouring out, all over her bedroom floor, just as she walked in.

I GULPED.

CHAPTER 7

I thought I was going to get through the day

without any

Until lunchtime, that is.

Daniel bounded up to Charlie and me

and said, "The new kid and the

weird kid sitting together. How

'NICE.'"

He said "nice" in a different way than when people normally say it. I wondered if it was sarcasm, but my sarcasm detector isn't very good. I can get confused when people say things all

⬆UPSIDE
DOWN⬇.

I tried to figure out if Daniel wasn't actually as bad as Charlie had warned and he *did* think it was nice that we were sitting together, or if he was being mean, because it obviously wasn't very nice of him to call Charlie

"the weird kid."

Anyway, Mom and Dad say to always think about things before blurting them out.

I could feel Charlie trying to think of what to say, too. He was taking air into his lungs really deeply, as if he was preparing to say something, and then opening his mouth and closing it again, but nothing came out.

I think we were both silent for a super-long time, which seemed to make Daniel very angry. He shouted,

before walking away.

When he was gone, Charlie said, "See? He's always horrible to me."

"Why?" I asked. "Did you two have a fight about something?"

"No. He just hates me for no reason. I think he hates the whole class, but he hates me the most."

Charlie looked so sad, and so small, I couldn't help putting my arm around him, which made Charlie look at me and smile his

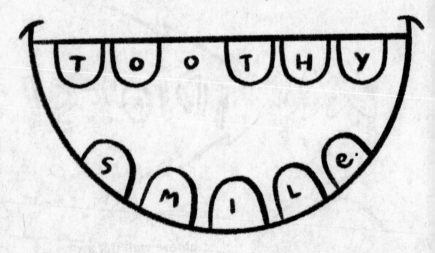

When Mom picked me up later, I told her

all about my new friend. I saw her breathe a

"phew." I guess she was worried about how

good or not good my first day would be since

I was so nervous. I also told her that I liked

Mrs. Hutchinson and her

amazing changing haiR.

Mom told me about her day, too. It

sounded like she'd had a great time at her

dream job, poking at MicRoscopic stuff

with fancy equipment. And on the way home

she'd passed a chocolate shop, so she bought

some for our neighbor to say hello properly.

Thankfully, she had bought one of those

fancy adult chocolate boxes with lots of dark

chocolates in it, which are so yuck that I didn't

wish the box was for me instead, which I

normally do when we have to give chocolate to

other people.

"I thought we could pop over when we get

home!"

"OK," I said slowly, remembering how grumpy

the neighbor had been last time I saw her.

We picked up Maryam and the

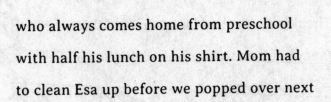

little human thing we call a brother,

who always comes home from preschool

with half his lunch on his shirt. Mom had

to clean Esa up before we popped over next

door, because she's embarrassed to have messy kids.

She even said to me, "Wait. Let me hair your run through my fingers."

ha ha ha ha ha! °ᴗ°

Mom says things the wrong way around when she's hurrying.

"You mean *run your fingers through his hair*," said Maryam, because she likes to correct people.

"Yes, yes, that," said Mom, and she marched us all over and took a deep breath and rang the doorbell.

We waited.

NOTHING!

We waited some more.

NOTHING!

So I reached forward and rapped on the door, really loud, a few times.

"Why did you do that?" Mom hissed like a quiet, angry snake.

"What?" I shrugged. "Maybe the doorbell isn't working?"

"Well, it's rude," hissed snake-Mom, and just then the door opened quietly and eerily, like in horror movies.

There stood an old lady. Quite a short one. With lots of white hair and one of those cardigans that all old ladies wear. My grandma has one.

We all said "Hi" pretty much together, except Esa, who said,

"Assalamu alaikum"

like he had been taught to say to our nani.

The old lady was really weird, because she

just stood there without reacting. She didn't say hello. She just stared.

Mom explained that we were the new neighbors.

The old lady stared.

Mom said, "We just thought we'd come over to introduce ourselves."

The old lady stared.

Maryam gave me a secret whack on the arm, which was meant to say:

OMG. THIS IS SO AWKWARD!

I gave her a secret whack back, which was meant to say:

OMG. I KNOW!

Then Mom asked the creepy, rude next-door neighbor what her name was.

Just when we thought she wouldn't say

anything, she blurted out, "Rogers," then slammed the door.

I glanced up at Mom. She looked like one of those helium balloons that hardly has any helium left in it at all.

CHAPTER 8

For a few mornings, as we left for school, my mom asked me if I had done my duas. My mom is absolutely

OBSESSED

with having a routine that we stick to every morning—a bit like it's one of her science experiments.

My parents do their duas whenever they think of something they want to talk to Allah about. I sometimes wonder if other people see a Muslim's lips moving and think they're

✦SECRETLY ✦CASTING✦
✦A SPELL✦

or just talking to themselves, when actually

they're just doing one of their duas.

There are duas for everything:

eating SLeePiNG

WAKiNG uP

PROTECTIÖN

knowledge

leaving the house 🏠◐
coming back into the house 🏠◐

Basically, anything you can think of.

I used to forget them sometimes, but now I was making sure I did them as soon as I woke up. Especially the prayer for

because Daniel was getting meaner every day and I felt like I needed all the help I could get.

He had started to follow Charlie and me around the playground at recess. Sometimes he wouldn't say anything, but he would do lots of staring and make grunting noises, as if he was having some really mean thoughts.

And once,

HE CHARGED AT US LIKE A RHINO.

Then he started laughing like mad because it made Charlie jump.

Minus Daniel, school was getting to be quite all right, especially since Charlie and me were becoming super-best friends. We laughed at all the same things, and we even wished for all the same things, like getting an Xbox and more screen time to go with it. That was starting to make up for how much I missed my friends back at my old school. I was still a bit worried that they might be forgetting about me, but Dad said we could all get together in the summer.

Mrs. Hutchinson was really nice, too. Every time she saw me in the mornings, or when she walked past my desk, she checked on me and gave me a **WiNK !**

Not all the lessons were fun, obviously, but whenever we did something creative, she got really enthusiastic and her curls were happy and bouncy. It made me wonder if maybe she could imagine things the way I did, or if she was just like all the other adults.

One afternoon, when we were doing an art lesson about Picasso, Mrs. Hutchinson was so excited about how he made everything abstract that her curls started dancing with joy. She asked us to paint self-portraits just like his.

Charlie and I were having loads of fun giving

ourselves colorful triangle noses and weird-

shaped eyes, when Daniel walked past our desk

and sent the dirty water cup tumbling onto my

painting.

"Oops, clumsy me . . ."

There he was again with the upside-down

talking. It definitely wasn't an *oops* moment, it

was a

Charlie's mouth dropped open in surprise

and my heart took a little dip, as if it was

falling into a different and less comfy place in my chest.

It seemed like Charlie could tell exactly how I was feeling. Because he leaned in to whisper, "He's just a big

FR☺GSPAWN

head. I bet you can paint a new one even better!" And he gave me the biggest toothy grin I'd seen yet.

I imagined what Picasso looked like. I wondered if he looked like some of his paintings, all out of shape, but happy. Happier than all the other paintings from those old days. And then I thought,

HEY, WHAT IF SOME KID HAD RUINED PICASSO'S PAINTING AT SCHOOL ONE DAY, WHICH IS WHY IT CAME OUT ALL DIFFERENT AND WEIRD, AND THAT'S WHAT MADE HIM FAMOUS?

So I took my paintbrush, I grabbed it like it was alive and like it was the first time I ever held a paintbrush, and I painted.

When Mrs. Hutchinson saw my work, her
curls almost rose to the ceiling.

"Omar, Omar," she said.

"Yes, Mrs. Hutchinson."

"It's . . . wow. It's brilliant!"

Daniel's face was red. Like the beets my dad
will never eat. He passed me a note.

It said:

When Mom came to pick me up, he stared at us both as if we were someone's old

chewing gum

that he had accidentally touched under the desk. I almost pointed him out to her, but then I remembered how relieved she'd been that I thought school was OK, and I kept quiet.

Sometimes, though, I think my mom magically knows when somebody in her family needs cheering up, because that evening she announced she was making biryani.

Biryani is my all-time favorite Pakistani food.

It's hard to make and Mom says scientists with full-time jobs don't have the time to make it every week, like I had asked her to.

Mom always opens the French doors to the patio when she is cooking, no matter how cold it is outside, because she can't stand the house smelling like food. Homes are meant to smell like nothing, she says,

NOT FISH,

NOT SAMOSAS,

NOT SMELLY SOCKS,

and not even weird, artificial air fresheners.
And since the door was open, I stood there with
my giant bubble kit to see if I could really make
a bubble bigger than me, like it said on the box.

I could see our next-door neighbor, the
horrible Mrs. Rogers. She was outside, poking
around at her weeds with one wrinkly hand and
holding her phone with the other.

After a few minutes, we heard her say
loudly:

"Oh, I'm with her on this one," joked Dad, who hates it when the smell of frying onion and garlic gets into his clothes.

"I know, I knowwwww. We don't want to give her another reason not to like us!" said Mom. Then she held Dad's arm, like she does when she is going to tell him a really good idea.

"Let's send her some! She'll love it! ♡"

I know it gets really stinky when the biryani is cooking, but SERIOUSLY, it's so yummy. It's worth it! I couldn't believe that Mom was being so nice after the way Mrs. Rogers treated us when we took her those chocolates. Why did she deserve some of our delicious dinner?

And to make it worse, Mom and Dad made Maryam and me take it over to her house. She took forever to open the door, as usual. And when she finally did and we tried to give her the container, she just said, "Spicy food??? No thank you!" as she closed the door.

"Sheeeeeeesh," said Maryam. "You'd think we were trying to poison her."

CHAPTER 9

Mom and Dad were so happy that I was doing

well at school that they said I could invite

Charlie over. They obviously didn't know the

bit about me not actually doing well at school

100% because Daniel made most

days **40%** bad. Well, depending on how

much he felt like a big, huge grump that day,

he sometimes made them **60%** bad.

I wondered why he was worse on some

days and I imagined him walking to school

and slipping on **ROTTEN APPLES.**

If you've ever seen a rotten apple, you'll know that they're really slimy and soft and can make you fall right down if you ever step on one, even more than a banana peel. So, the more rotten apples he slipped on, the worse he felt, and the more mean he was. That could be it. **THERE HAD TO BE SOMETHING.**

Charlie was mega excited about coming over. I asked him if he wanted to have pizza and he said yes, which is what I knew he would say, because every kid loves pizza. (Unless they're allergic to cheese, like my cousin Faiza, who does lots of farts and gets really bad tummy aches if she eats it.)

Charlie told me all about the flavors that he hates tasting in food, but luckily none of them are on pizzas:

Charlie was very polite to my mom and dad when he came over. He said extra pleases and thank-yous. And he smiled an extra lot.

"I've been hearing so much about you, Charlie," said Mom.

"Oh, thank you," said Charlie.

"It's so nice to have you over, and you can come anytime you want," said Dad.

THEY WERE BEING SO CHEESY.

I imagined them as blocks of cheese, the holey kind that they draw in cartoons but which I've never actually tasted.

Maryam decided to hang out near us and show off like she always does. The weird thing about it was that Charlie actually *liked* her.

She even came with us to play soccer in the

backyard. She used to play soccer normally, but recently she's started giggling a lot and celebrating with loud

It's super annoying. Charlie didn't seem to mind, though. He laughed right along with her, the way he does with me, but not really with many other people in the class.

All this laughing made Mrs. Rogers come into her backyard to investigate. She must have been on the phone, because she was talking to the person called John again.

She said it very loudly.

"I mean really, why can't they play quietly like good children? I can't take this much ridiculous noise."

We all looked at each other, suddenly silent. We couldn't see her face over the fence, just the top of her white hair. And then we burst out laughing and ran inside to eat our pizza.

CHAPTER 10

At school, it was getting harder and harder to avoid **Daniel Green.**

One lunchtime, he came over and put a handful of sand all over my food. My stomach clenched and I got a lump in my throat. I didn't want to cry in front of him, but I was really hungry, and that sandwich, from last night's leftover chicken, was really tasty and my mouth had really been looking forward to it.

I quickly imagined H_2O swooping down from the clouds to hover right behind Daniel. I made H_2O pull a totally unimpressed face and blow steam all over Daniel's head. And Daniel had no clue.

That made me laugh and through my giggles

I said loudly, **"Thanks, Daniel. Now I truly have a sand-wich."**

A few people around us started laughing, too. Sarah and Ellie—girls from our class—were sitting at the lunch table next to ours, and they were giggling like crazy.

Daniel stood there towering over me with his fists closed tight. His face was redder than his T-shirt, and he was **CLENCHING HIS TEETH**

together tightly. I pictured him as a Rottweiler dog, baring his sharp teeth, ready for a fight.

At this point I realized that being smart with a bully wasn't very smart at all. Charlie must have realized this, too, because he had been sensible enough not to laugh and now he looked like a frightened little lamb.

I quickly muttered the

dua under my breath.

Then there was a loud growling sound and Daniel was launching his head toward my stomach. I don't know how, but I managed to throw myself onto the floor out of his way. It was all very fast. Daniel's head went into my empty chair, with his huge body following. The force sent the chair flying into the girls behind us, followed by a

VERY BIG, VERY ANGRY

body that ended up on top of Sarah.

I probably don't need to tell you that

Daniel was in **BIG FAT TROUBLE.**

He spent one hour in Mr. Barnes's class as

punishment. Mr. Barnes has a mustache. A big

one. It looks
like it could
come alive on
his face like a

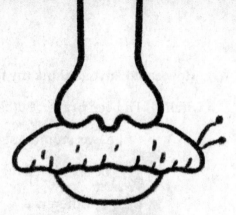

SLITHERING
SLUG.

At the end of the day, Daniel was back. He still looked angry. As we lined up to leave the classroom, he stood behind me and breathed down my neck.

"Don't think I don't know the worst thing about you. YOU'RE MUSLIM. I saw your mom the other day, looking like a witch, in black. You better go back to your country before we kick you all out."

I didn't say a word. I just gulped.

How could anyone think my mom looked like a witch? If I'd been braver, I'd have told Daniel he was stupid not to be able to tell the difference.

eats kids for dinner	would never harm a kid
poisonous wart	wart, if present, is not poisonous
has no hair under wig	has lots of hair under scarf
scowl 😠	♥ smile ♥ (.ᵕ.)
ugly, due to evil thoughts	beautiful, due to lovely thoughts

On the way home, I couldn't stop thinking about what Daniel had said.

BEFORE THEY KICK US ALL OUT? WHAAAAT?

I thought about talking to Maryam about him. Maybe she could help and tell me what to do, without having to tell our parents. I know they'd get all stressy and worried and make a big fuss at school and that would definitely just make Daniel worse. Maryam might be annoying, but she used to stand up for me back when I was a really little kid and we still went to the same school . . .

But then I remembered the time just before we moved when I was quietly trying to get away with going over my screen time limit in my room and Dad came stomping in, like a giant who had just stepped on an enormous thumbtack.

I COULD PRACTICALLY SEE THE STEAM COMING OUT OF HIS EARS.

He had discovered the TV remote was missing its batteries. I froze. I didn't move and didn't say a word. I imagined I was a spider playing dead when someone is trying to smack it with a slipper.

Then Maryam came in with her huge, pointy finger of accusation.

HE DID IT!

It was true. I had desperately needed them for my controller . . .
I got into so much trouble that day. I was banned from video games for a month.

Maryam is a complete snitch these days. No, I couldn't trust her.

CHAPTER 11

I knew there was one person I *could* trust to
talk to about Daniel: my cousin Reza. And
luckily, we were going up to Manchester to
visit a couple of days after the sand disaster.
I was bursting to ask him whether he'd heard
about Muslims getting kicked out of the
country. Did Daniel just make that part up?
Could it possibly be real?

REZA is SUPER COOL.

He's twelve. He's the kind of kid that knows
a lot about everything. If anything happens

to his bike, he can fix it using his dad's tools, and I've even seen him changing the oil in his mom's little red car, which he calls a clunker. And when we walk around in Manchester with him and his family, lots of people always say, "Hi." Reza must have really great pester power skills, or maybe he knows hypnosis, because he literally has everything he wants. That's one of the reasons I love going there: because we have two days of playing on his Xbox as much as we want and we always have a

midnight feast.

YUM!

I'm pretty sure almost every Muslim has cousins in Manchester. I was wondering if they were all as interesting as mine while I finished packing my backpack, when my dad shouted up the stairs, "Get in the Peanut, everyone! We're leaving in two minutes!"

You might be wondering how we could all get into a peanut. We can't. This is what we call the **PEANUT.** It's a 4x4. But look at the license plate!

There are some things that always happen on our road trip to Manchester:

- ⦿ Mom packs too much food foR the jouRney
- ⦿ Dad complains when he is puttinG the LuGGaGe in the caR
- ⦿ we alwaYs stoP at the Rest aReA and eat HoT food, So mom's jouRney food is uneaten
- ⦿ Dad saYs,

"I TOLD YOU SO."

As we were loading the car with all our stuff, Mrs. Rogers came out into her front yard to put a bag in the garbage can.

But instead of just going back inside, she

stood and watched us with

I waved at her and gave her my best smile, just

to see what would happen. She gave me her

best blank expression.

SHE MUST BE THE MEANEST PERSON ON THE PLANET AFTER DANIEL GREEN.

When we were on the highway, Esa started saying he needed to pee.

"But it's only been forty minutes!" said Dad.

Mom said, "I knew I shouldn't have given you that apple juice."

Dad said he had to hold it until we got to the rest area. But Mom said he was only little and couldn't hold it that long. Maryam said, "We should have put a diaper on him because he's a big fat baby."

Dad said to stop being so rude.

I hate it when we are stuck in the car and everyone is being all stressed out and I also hate the thought of Esa peeing on the seat right next to me. I mean, how

YUCK!

I would end up sitting in a

puddle of his pee.

So I stared out of the window and imagined myself on my Rollerblades, riding alongside all the cars and faster than them. So fast that there was

A JET OF FIRE

blazing out the

back of them.

And then I said,

ROLLERBLADES lift off!

And they took me all the way to the moon.

I don't actually have any Rollerblades, and

I don't know how to roller-skate, but that's

the great thing about imagining: you can do

anything you want. Except pee. For that, we

had to stop on the shoulder of the road so

Esa could let it out.

I asked my parents why it was called

the shoulder. Nobody knew. This is why

my parents should let me have my own

smartphone, because then I could have

just looked it up myself.

That night, while we pretended to be asleep
on our row of mattresses on Aunty Sumayyah's
living room floor, Reza told me that Daniel was
right, we were all going to be kicked
out of the country and we
were probably going
to have a

WORLD WAR III.

I gulped. He told me that we would all have to
go and live in Pakistan.

"Have you ever been to Pakistan?" I said.

"Yeah. Once, when I was five."

"What's it like? Will we like living there?"

I felt sick. **I didn't want to live in a strange place I had never been to.**

The five bars of chocolate that we had snuck into our beds and eaten attempted to make their way back up my throat.

"Well, the pizza is

and you can hardly understand what people are saying," Reza said.

"Why?"

"Because they speak in Urdu. You can't speak Urdu, can you?"

"No."

I lay awake for ages after Reza had fallen asleep. I imagined his quiet snoring sounds were from H_2O instead and that my pillow was resting on H_2O's back. It made me feel better to know that wherever we had to move to, I could take him with me.

At breakfast, there was such a big feast of food on the table that I forgot all about Daniel and Pakistan. Uncle Fahad had even pulled out last night's leftover chicken wings.

What's that? asked Esa.

Meat, said Dad.

Where did it come from?

A chicken.

Did it lay it?

Everyone burst into laughter. Uncle Fahad

choked on his juice.

CHAPTER 12

One evening the following week, when we were

putting our lasagna-covered dishes into the

dishwasher, we heard an

coming down our street. Maryam and I both

raced to the window, while Esa whined to be

let down from the table (he was still eating, as

usual, because he's super slow).

The ambulance lights were flashing
so brightly the whole room was lit up.

Maryam and I pressed our faces to the glass. The ambulance had stopped next door and the paramedics were hurrying toward the front door.

"It's Mrs. Rogers!" I said in surprise.

"Oh no . . ." gasped Mom.

Dad had his quick-thinking face on.

"I should go," said Mom. "Should I go? I should go."

Maryam said, "No way, she's horrible!"

Esa dropped his plate of freezing-cold lasagna on the floor with a

Dad looked at it and breathed a sigh and ran his hand through his hair. He does that when he has his thinking face on.

"What if she doesn't want me? What if she sends me away and shouts at me in front of them?" Mom said as she ran around the room putting her scarf on her head and putting her coat on inside out.

"It doesn't matter, darling. You go. At least you will have done the right thing. Go and see if she needs anything at all."

"She doesn't deserve it,"

said Maryam and she folded her arms and threw herself onto the sofa.

I went to the front door and watched as

Mom hurried out of our gate. She reached the ambulance just as they were wheeling Mrs. Rogers out on a stretcher. She was clutching her wrist and telling the paramedics how she had slipped in the bathroom.

"I'm here with you," Mom said softly. "I mean, if you want." And then Mom put her hand out so Mrs. Rogers could hold it if she wanted.

Mrs. Rogers looked really pale and scared. She said in a small voice, "John isn't here."

And then she took Mom's hand and tried to

smile.

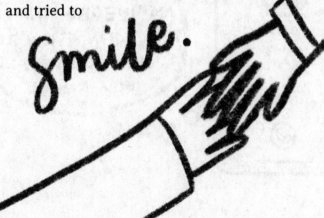

Later, Mom said that when Mrs. Rogers did that, it was easy to forget all about the rotten things that she had said.

When Mom and Mrs. Rogers came home in a taxi a few hours later, Dad went over, too, to help Mrs. Rogers get settled. When they came back, he was grinning from ear to ear because he had heard Mrs. Rogers on the phone as they were leaving, saying,

CHAPTER 13

All we seemed to talk about in our house for
the next little while was how Mrs. Rogers was
doing.

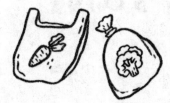

**Does Mrs. Rogers
need anything from
the supermarket?**

**Should Omar pop over
and check Mrs. Rogers's
TV is working properly?**

**Should Esa pick some
flowers from the garden
to cheer Mrs. Rogers up?**

Now that Mrs. Rogers knew we were nice,

she was a **TOTALLY DIFFERENT PERSON.**

She wasn't **CREEPY** and **MEAN**

anymore. She was **✽ Super Happy ✽**

whenever we went over to her house. That

made me wonder why she didn't like us in the

first place. Could it be because the fall made

her brain work differently? When I suggested

this to Dad, he laughed and said that although

that was possible, he thought it had more to do with what she had been reading before in the tabloid newspapers about Muslims, where now she knew what we were really like. He said we should invite her to our house during Ramadan so she could learn more about the real Islam.

Adults get super excited about Ramadan,

which is kind of confusing because during Ramadan you can't eat or drink ALL DAY. I know my mom and dad like to eat a whole lot, and my mom is completely addicted to coffee. Even though they make up for all the not eating when they break their fast at iftar time, no one had ever really explained to me what was so good about Ramadan. So I asked Aunty Iman.

Aunty Iman was my new Qur'an teacher. She isn't related to us, but Maryam and I call all ladies that are our mom's age "Aunty" because it's rude to just say their name. She comes over to teach me how to read the Qur'an every Wednesday and Friday after school. I like her because she's kind. She's

than my last teacher from before we moved, who didn't tell me about what the words meant and just told me to be quiet whenever I asked a question about Allah, which made it boring. I like to know what the words mean. I heard my mom telling my dad that the teacher wasn't doing a good job of handling my

INQUISITIVE NATURE.

Anyway, it was super handy that Aunty Iman filled me in on what's so good about Ramadan, because Charlie has an inquisitive nature, too, and he started asking me lots of questions all about it.

"So, wait, Omar, in Ramadan, you can't eat for a whole month? Won't people die if they do that?" he asked.

"Hahahaha. No. You only have to stop eating

From dawn till sunset.

Basically, when the sun is out. All the other times, you can eat what you want, and you can eat lots, like my mom and dad do, so you stay alive."

"OK." Charlie looked a bit relieved but a bit sheepish, too, so I felt a little bad for laughing. "But why do people do it? The fasting, I mean. And if they like doing it, why do they only do it in Ramadan?"

"Because that's when you're supposed to do it, and for a whole month you get extra reward points from Allah. I found out that you get seventy times more points for praying and reading the Qur'an than you do in other months." We were sitting by the sandbox in the playground, so I made two piles with the sand, one that was like a

MASSIVE MOUNTAIN

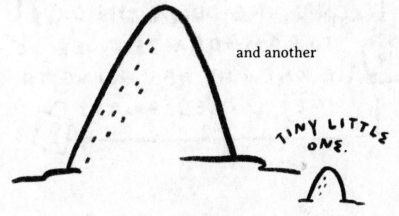

and another

TINY LITTLE ONE.

"OK. That's really cool," said Charlie. "Is it hard?"

"I think so. Anyway, even if it's hard, we have the ꙭ Ëid feast ꙮ to look forward to at the end of the month! It also helps that the Devil is locked up during Ramadan, so he can't persuade us to eat when our tummies are rumbling."

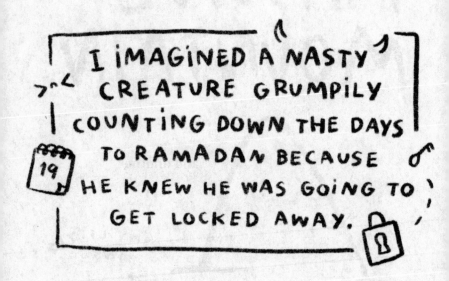

I IMAGINED A NASTY CREATURE GRUMPILY COUNTING DOWN THE DAYS TO RAMADAN BECAUSE HE KNEW HE WAS GOING TO GET LOCKED AWAY.

And since it's the Devil who whispers to us to do bad things, I was pretty relieved that I could have a whole month without him telling me to eat Maryam's stash of hidden chocolate when she wasn't looking.

I was planning to ask Allah for a lifetime's supply of chocolate of my own on the

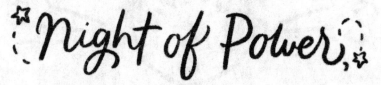

which is in the last ten days of Ramadan. It's called that because it's better than

months. That means you could get the same reward points in one night that it would take you one thousand months to get! That's eighty-

three years!

MIND-BLOWING!

WOW!

And all the angels come down to Earth and you

can ask Allah for anything you want.

Then I remembered the best part. "AND for

people who fast, Allah will give them a secret

reward and we don't know what it is!"

"Wow," said Charlie. "Maybe like a **FERRARI** or something?"

"OH MY GOSH, Charlie! That would be so awesome." I could almost feel the steering wheel in my hands . . .

CHAPTER 14

The first fast was on a Monday. Maryam was going to wake up for the MIDNIGHT FEAST! because she was going to be fasting for the whole of Ramadan for the first time. The meal is called suhur, and it has to happen before dawn. My mom said that I wasn't allowed to get up for it because I was still too young. I wasn't happy about this at all—I wanted my Ferrari! So I put up a fuss and turned on the turbo on my

PESTER POWER.

In the end, Mom said I could practice keeping a fast on the weekend. I said fine, but I was still worried about Maryam getting more reward points than me.

So I went to school with breakfast in my tummy as usual. It was funny that at school it was just a normal day, when at home it was special because it was the first day of Ramadan and that's all that anyone could talk about. Nobody in my class was talking about it, which is why I was super surprised when Mrs. Hutchinson bounced over to my table and said,

"Happy Ramadan, Omar."

I think my cheeks might have gone red. But I looked at her, at her Happy Ramadan curls, and managed a very small thank-you.

"Are you fasting?" she continued, crouching down near my chair.

"No, I'm not allowed," I said.

"Oh, well," she said, "I'm happy to go easy on you for PE if you ever do." And she winked and went to write the date on the board.

The first person I saw when I looked up was Daniel.

Something was making him red, and fidgety, and really angry.

Could it have been jealousy?

At break time, Daniel came over to where Charlie and I were sitting, doing cool graffiti drawings with chalks on the floor.

"YOU'RE A TEACHER'S PET!" He spat out the words as if they were a really nasty part of a pet, like its poop. And he pointed his finger at me, back and forth, back and forth, before smudging up our drawings with his foot.

Anger bubbled up in my chest.

I imagined H_2O swooping down from the clouds and whacking Daniel with his strong tail.

If only he could do that for real . . . I was so tired of Daniel using any old excuse to pick on me.

"GO AWAY, DANIEL," I said.

"What will you do? Call your *girlfriend*, Mrs. Hutchinson?"

"She's not his girlfriend, OK?" said Charlie.

For a second, I thought Daniel was going to try his headbutting thing again, but luckily, he saw one of the teaching assistants coming toward us, so he ran away. The teaching assistant walked past us slowly, asking if everything was all right. I said yes, even though it wasn't.

Afterward, Charlie asked me if we should just go and tell her or Mrs. Hutchinson that Daniel was being a big fat bully. I just shook my head. I knew getting Daniel in trouble would only make things worse. But I also knew that I had to do *something*—standing up to Daniel made me feel shaky and sick, and I super definitely didn't want to have to feel that way forever.

I imagined H_2O flying off into the distance and entering a big fluffy white cloud in the blue sky. I decided that's where he lives. Everyone's seen it—it's the big cloud that is shaped like a dragon. It probably feels like being wrapped up in

cotton balls

like the ones my mom uses on her face. If the cloud wasn't there and the sky was clear blue, it would be because H_2O had gone to visit his friends or buy some

or whatever dragons do in their spare time when their owners don't need them. And when the cloud was darker and spilled rain onto the earth, that would be when H_2O was taking

a shower.

YOU DIDN'T THINK DRAGONS NEEDED TO WASH?

Well, maybe your dragon doesn't see as much

action as my H_2O...

CHAPTER 15

That evening, Mrs. Rogers came over for the first iftar, which is the food you eat when you break your fast at sunset. Her wrist still wasn't all better yet, and Mom and Dad had been sending dinner over to her so that she didn't have to cook for herself. But this was the first time she actually came to eat at our house, at our table.

She watched everything we did, quietly, with a smile in her eyes. She kept saying,

I SEE!

and nodding her head.

Once we'd finished eating, she took her phone out and called John—who was her son, it turned out—and said, "The Muslims put less chili in their food for me, John. It was *delicious*." We all grinned, because being called "The Muslims" was a bit of a fun joke for us all now.

As the week went on, I noticed that everyone was getting used to not eating when the sun was out. And actually eating a bit too much when the sun went down. Normally, Maryam and I eat about the same amount, but now

SHE WAS EATING LIKE A BEAR WHO HADN'T HAD ANY FOOD FOR THE WHOLE TIME IT HAD BEEN HIBERNATING.

At first, I was worried that she would eat all the ~~yummy samosas~~ if I wasn't quick enough, but then I figured out that while she was busy munching, I could talk loads about my video games and she wouldn't tell me to shut up like she normally does.

Mrs. Rogers came over for the iftar every day. She told me she liked the samosas best of all.

But by the time we got to Thursday, everyone was a little bit less patient. Probably because they were hungry. It didn't help that Maryam had done really badly on her science test, which was a

COMPLETE CATASTROPHE ☒

in our household because she is the daughter of two successful scientists. Mom was telling her that it really wasn't good enough and that they would go over all the things that she found hard. And Dad was saying that they wouldn't be upset if they didn't believe that Maryam could do better.

I looked at Maryam. Once, I watched a video of a gorilla dad whose gorilla children were being really, really annoying, and he  was trying his best to be patient and not to "go ape," until he DID. Maryam reminded me of the gorilla, trying to stay calm. It didn't last long.

"WELL, iT'S NOT MY FAULT,
iS iT? YOU'RE THE ONE wHO
MADE ME MOVE TO THiS STUPiD
SCHOOL AND STUPiD HOUSE!"
SHOUTED GORiLLA-MARYAM.

"Mommy, I can do better, can't I?" said Esa.

"Of course you can, sweetie," said Mom.

For this, Maryam pinched Esa as she stormed

out of the room. Mom was a bit flustered and

didn't seem to notice, but I kept quiet about

it because **i might be able
to use it against her in
the future.**

Mom said I was sitting around doing nothing,

so I should go and set the table for iftar and

take the stones out of the middle of the dates

and put nuts in instead. I wondered why they were called stones and I imagined what would happen if there were real stones in dates and somebody tried to eat one, thinking it had a nut in it. If they didn't smash their teeth doing that and managed to swallow it instead, would it stay in their tummies forever, or would they poop it out?

Just as I had finished setting the table, Dad came into the room. He liked that I had gone over the top and taken out fancy glasses and made the table look like they do in restaurants. Mom put her head around the door. She didn't like it. She said that her fancy glasses could get broken and that I shouldn't touch them. Then she told me to go and get Mrs. Rogers to join us for iftar.

Mrs. Rogers brought a box of chocolates with her.

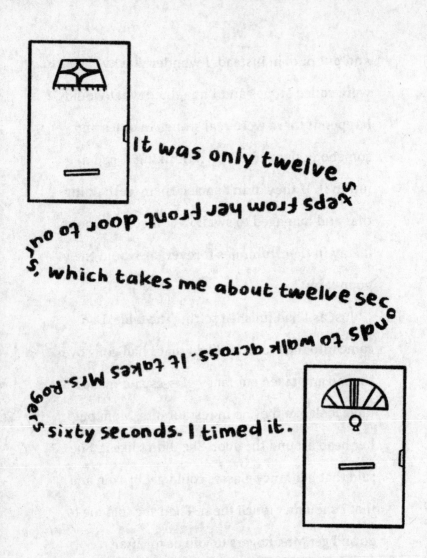

It was only twelve steps from her front door to ours, which takes me about twelve seconds to walk across. It takes Mrs. Rogers sixty seconds. I timed it.

That doesn't sound like a lot, but it's really slow when you're doing it with her. While we

walked, I had my eye on the chocolates. How could I make sure that Maryam didn't steal all the best ones?

Mrs. Rogers knew the iftar routine now. When there were only ten minutes left till the fast opened, she said, "Put the Islam Channel on, or we'll miss that nice song that tells us when the fast opens."

We all tried not to look at each other and tried not to laugh.

"That's called the adhan, Mrs. Rogers," said Dad. "It's the call to prayer."

"Oh, well, whatever it's called, it's very nice, dear," said Mrs. Rogers.

Mrs. Rogers did the countdown, and everyone popped a date into their mouths when the fast opened. EXCEPT ME!

I popped a chocolate from the box that Mrs. Rogers had brought into my mouth. Because my mouth had been waiting for them. And because my mouth likes chocolates very much. But instead of being very happy, my mouth was confused. There was a

WEIRD TASTE

with the chocolate taste. I didn't like it.

"YUCK!" I said.

"Oh! Is it an alcohol one?" said Maryam.

WHAAAA

We're not allowed alcohol, not even the adults, and I had never had it before.

I quickly jumped up to spit it out and rinse my mouth.

"Am I going to be drunk now?" I asked.

Apparently, this was totally hilarious, because you have to have a lot more alcohol than that to get drunk. Mrs. Rogers explained that to me after she finished laughing for ten minutes straight.

AAAAT?!

CHAPTER 16

When Friday evening finally came around, I was very excited. I had somehow made it to the weekend without getting my bones broken by Daniel AND I was going to be fasting the next day, which meant

I was one step closer to my

FERRARI.

I knew I had to wake up at two o'clock in the morning to eat before sunrise. That's

basically the

middle of the night.

At first, I couldn't even sleep because I was too excited about getting up when I normally wouldn't be allowed to.

But the next thing I knew, Maryam was waking me up by saying,

"GET UP, BRAT FACE,"

and poking me in the ribs with long fingers and, for some weird reason, blowing on my face, complete with added bits of spit!

Was SHAYTAN still whispering to her somehow and making her be mean?

It took me a moment to remember why I

wasn't supposed to be asleep, but then I jumped
out of bed.

MIDNIGHT FEAST!

I whizzed down the stairs and jumped
onto my seat at the table in the kitchen.
Then I jumped right back up to get my
favorite cereal.

"How are you this perky, this early in the
morning?" said something that sounded a bit
like Dad.

Mom and Dad looked different. Like half
zombies. They weren't speaking very much,
and when they did, it was just one or two
words, and it was a bit slurred.

"Mm, eggs?"

(Usually said as "Would you like some eggs?")

"H-hot..."

(Usually said as "Be careful—it's hot!")

They were also moving a lot slower than normal. I imagined it was because the whole room was filled with **thick**

zombie
SLIME

and they were wading through it in slow motion.

Adults are funny—I can't understand why they have different levels of energy depending on how much sleep or coffee they've had. I'm basically the same all the time. I think Maryam is on her way to being an adult, because she was at least a quarter zombie while we were eating suhur.

I had some cereal and was forced to have some egg and porridge, too (with hazelnut spread, obviously). Then we all went back to bed.

When I woke up on Saturday morning, I had to remember not to eat breakfast and

not to dRink oR eat anything.

I was doing fine till about noon, when my tummy started to rumble a bit. I ignored it and tried to distract myself by building a Lego Triceratops. It worked, because the

 went away and by the time Dad announced that

we had to get into the Peanut to go to the supermarket, I had forgotten all about hunger.

That was until we actually reached the supermarket, and I saw all the shelves stacked with

CHOCOLATE CROISSANTS

AND WAFFLES

AND CAKES.

Even the things I don't normally eat, like quiche, sat on shelves looking more yummy than they ever did before. My tummy growled like

H_2O. My insides suddenly ached, and my legs pretended to be noodles.

On the drive back, I asked Dad if I could break my fast. He said that I could, because I was just a kid, and at least I had tried. He said there was a reason why Allah said that

KiDS DON'T HAVE TO FAST. 👍

Their bodies aren't like adult bodies.

"But are you sure that Allah won't mind?" I asked.

He said of course Allah wouldn't mind
and that Allah would just be happy that I had
wanted to try in the first place.

"You can always try again next weekend, if
you like."

That made me happy. I took a chocolate
croissant out of the bag next to me and took a
big bite.

Just for the record,
I did try again next
weekend, and I kept
a whole fast. I've been
looking forward to my
: FERRARI : ever since.

CHAPTER 17

We'd been living in our new house for seven

whole weeks. That doesn't sound like a lot, but

it was weird:

MY BEDROOM  REALLY FELT LIKE MY BEDROOM NOW.

Even though when I shut
my eyes I could still
remember exactly
how my old

room looked, with the stickers on the dresser that were peeling off, and the glow-in-the-dark stars on the ceiling that Dad helped me put up when I was younger, and Esa's teddies all over the floor. I didn't feel like I wanted to move back. I liked pretty much everything about where we lived now.

Everything except . . . Can you guess? **Daniel** obviously.

Nobody else seemed to have a problem with me, but Daniel kept ruining everything. Most of our class hung out together on the playground, and though Charlie was my best friend, we often played soccer with Filip and Jayden and Jessica. Once or twice, the girls at the table next to ours asked for my help in science, *even* Sarah, who is smart at everything.

I'll give you an example of how Daniel made
me feel miserable about

A MILLION

pointless things. One Wednesday afternoon,
Mrs. Hutchinson asked a question. It was the
type of question that teachers ask when they
know that the kids won't know the answer, but
they ask it anyway, just to see.

She asked, "What is DNA?"

The class was blank. I knew Mrs. Hutchinson
had expected that because she didn't look
disappointed. I knew what it was, but I didn't
want to be a show-off.

"OK, does anybody know what genes are?"
she said.

One kid put his hand up and proudly said, "Clothes."

"No . . ." she said slowly, stretching it out, which meant she wanted other guesses.

"Genies?" asked another kid, clearly unsure.

Mrs. Hutchinson's face still smiled, but her hair and eyes gave it away. She was sad her class didn't have at least a clue about what genes were.

I COULDN'T TAKE IT ANYMORE. I SHOT MY HAND UP.

"Genes are what make us what we are. They're like special instructions. They decide what color our eyes are, and things like that. And DNA is where the genes are found. Lots of them!"

Mrs. Hutchinson's hair sprang to life, like flowers that had just been watered.

She said she was astonished at how much I knew about genes. I told her my parents were both scientists and it was one of their favorite topics.

Charlie gave me a high five.

But then Daniel gave me a **ROTTEN** look, and suddenly I wished I'd never said anything at all. Every time he glared at me, or pushed me and Charlie around on the playground, it reminded me of what he'd said—that

I SHOULD BE
= KICKED OUT =
OF MY HOME

AAH!

and sent to a country I'd never even visited. I
didn't *think* he could be right, but if he wasn't,
then why would Reza believe it was going to
happen, too?

At home things were just as normal.
Everyone was settled into the Ramadan
routine and starting to plan for Eid, which
was just around the corner. We have two Eids
in the year and they are the two best days of
the year for me. There's *Eid ul-Fitr*, which

was the Eid coming up, the one that is for celebrating that we've fasted for a whole month and earned lots of reward points. And then there is *Eid al-Adha* just a couple of months later, which basically celebrates Hajj—that's when people go to

Mecca

on a holy journey. We have to sacrifice a sheep or something on that Eid, like Prophet Abraham did, but obviously if you don't have a farm, you can't do it yourself.

If I had to choose, my favorite Eid is the first one, because that's when I seem to get

A WHOLE LOT MORE PRESENTS.

Maybe by the second one everyone's money has run out or something.

I usually drop a lot of hints to my parents about what presents to get me.

Pleeeeeeease can I have an Xbox One? Pleeease?

OK, maybe it's not hinting. Maybe it's begging.

My mom orders lots of the presents and Eid clothes online. But it's funny, because when the deliveryman comes, she runs around the house going AARRGGGHHH and looking for her headscarf. Which is never "where she left it." It usually involves her hopping from room to room before sprinting upstairs to grab one and opening the door panting and apologizing. Once or twice, she's even grabbed my hoodie and used it as a hijab.

The last time this happened, Maryam pointed out that people who aren't Muslim must think that Muslim women wear their scarves on their heads

ALL DAY LONG.

Even at home. Because whenever she comes to the door, Mom always has one on. They must think **Mom sleeps in it** and **showers in it** and **eats her breakfast** in it. When Maryam isn't being

Princess Grumpy-Pants

she can be really funny. The thought of Mom

showering in her headscarf had us laughing

for literally seven and a half minutes. I kept

imagining her shampooing it and blow-drying

it. And then at dinner, out of the blue, Maryam

blurted out,

"SHOWER SCARF!"

and I spat my food all over the table because I

laughed so hard.

CHAPTER 18

Have you ever gone on a school trip but never quite made it to where you were supposed to be going? If you haven't, you're lucky. Me?

My class was supposed to be going to the Science Museum. My parents were obviously extremely excited about this. The Science Museum had a new section called the

Wonderlab, which Mom and Dad took us to see as soon as it opened. But it was super cool, so I didn't mind going again. Especially because they have these slides made out of different materials, to teach you about friction, and one of them is really fast.

SO FAST THAT i ALMOST PEED MYSELF LAUGHiNG

the first time I went on it.

We were put into groups of six for the trip. A teaching assistant or a parent was in charge of each group. I could tell Mrs. Hutchinson was stressed that morning because some curls from her hair were looking pretty and in place, and others were sticking out in funny directions—completely ignoring gravity.

I listened as she read out names for the groups.

"MY HEART WAS THUDDING IN MY CHEST."

I had my fingers crossed under the table, because I really didn't want to be in Daniel's group. I knew I wasn't supposed to believe in crossing fingers. But I was trying anything. It was only later that I realized I didn't even ask Allah not to put me in Daniel's group. My mom said that if I had, Allah might have put me in a different group, or he might have even still put me in Daniel's group because He works in mysterious ways.

As you've probably guessed, I was put in a group with Daniel. And Charlie was in a whole different group.

When our names were announced, Daniel looked over at me and snarled. The worst part was that it wasn't even a teacher in charge of our group. It was just another kid's parent. And she had no idea which kids were

TROUBLEMAKERS

and which were not.

Charlie came up to me and said, "Don't

worry, OK? We can still look at things together
in the museum, OK?"

I said, "OK," too. I was feeling too miserable
to say anything else.

To get to the museum, we had to go on the
London Underground. It was going pretty all
right, until we tried to change trains.

DANIEL WAS LIKE
A LION WAITING
TO POUNCE.

As soon as we switched platforms, in the
rush of people, he took hold of the belt of my
pants and jerked me back.

"Your girlfriend, Charlie, can't save you
now," he barked.

Have you ever wanted to laugh in a
horrible situation? I don't know why, but

I CRACKED UP LAUGHING

even though I was probably about to get hit
by the worst bully I'd ever met. It was a weird
kind of not-real laugh, though, and it just
seemed to make Daniel more furious.

"Oh, so you think it's funny, do you, teacher's
pet?!"

People in dark suits and fancy shoes were
walking past us as if nothing out of the ordinary
was going on.

"Our group! The class! We'll get left
behind!" I finally managed to squeak.

Daniel looked over and saw what I saw:
a crowd of busy-looking people exiting the

platform, but nobody from our school. He seemed to freeze. Then, just a few seconds later, we were the only two people left.

What happened next was completely astonishing.

Daniel started wailing like a baby.

"WAAAAAA! WE'RE LOST. WE'RE GOING TO DIE."

I realized that I was going to have to handle this situation. And take care of the big crying bully baby in front of me even though Daniel was making me want to cry, too. I had been on the London Underground with my parents

millions of times. But never on my own. It

looked different now that I was on my own.

It looked bigger. Noisier. Darker. *Scarier.* And

it smelled like pee.

No, wait, that was Daniel.

He had peed himself.

CHAPTER 19

I know we should have tried to find somebody
who worked at the station to help, but my
thinking wasn't very straight at that time.
It was kind of WOBBLY and
I was getting
like a gazillion
different ideas
of what to do
every second.
That's a very
noisy head and,
don't forget,
Daniel was still
crying.

A train  RUMBLED ONTO THE PLATFORM

from the tunnel, and my instinct was to jump on.

Instincts are funny. You hear about them with animals, like when sea turtles hatch and move toward the ocean without anybody telling them which way to go. Or when baby kangaroos jump into their mommy kangaroo's pouch when they are born. I felt myself wanting to

 JUMP onto that

train, although nobody had told me it was the right way to go.

I took Daniel's hand, trying very hard not to think about when he had **picked his nose** earlier, and stepped on.

It was South Kensington station we were supposed to be going to. I remembered Mrs. Hutchinson saying so, and I remembered that when I went to the museum with Mom and Dad, we had to walk quite a lot through the station to get out near where the museums were.

Daniel and I found seats on the train.

"Do you know where to go?" sobbed Daniel.

"Yes, look on that map up there," I said, pointing toward the one that shows all the stops. "See if you can find South Kensington on it."

We looked. Very carefully. Marylebone

station came. We still searched the map, but

South Kensington was nowhere on that brown

line. My heart sank as I said to Daniel:

I think we have to change trains again.

I love the Peanut, but suddenly I wished that

we went to more places on the train so I would

know what I was doing.

"Let's tell someone we're lost," pleaded

Daniel.

"No. We're not lost," I said. I kind of knew

we were, but I wanted to get us out of the mess.

Now that Daniel was all sniffly and depending

on me, I wanted to be a

HERO.

"We just have to get off this train," I said.

"Then we'll be fine."

We got off at the next stop. It was Baker
Street. Baker Street sounded very familiar.
It sounded like home and good memories.
I thought maybe it was another station that
was close to the museums, and that's why I
remembered it.

Daniel was like a

BIG LUMP OF PLAY DOUGH

that couldn't think. I had to do all the thinking.

But it sort of felt OK—he wasn't being mean to

me anymore, at least.

I wondered whether our class knew we were

missing by now. I imagined Mrs. Hutchinson's

hair going wild with worry. I had never seen

her really worried before and I wondered what

it looked like.

We exited the station, crossed over at a

crosswalk and walked down a busy road with

lots of cafés on it. There was a Sherlock Holmes

museum. I don't know much about Sherlock, but

my parents always watch a TV show about him
that has Benedict Cumberbatch in it. Another
thing I know about Benedict Cumberbatch is that
he can't say the word "penguin." I only know this
because one time when I walked into the kitchen,
my mom was watching a video about him and
laughing so much that tears were falling from
her eyes.

The road started winding to the left, and
as we turned the corner, something touched
my shoulder from behind. I swung my head
around, and what I saw made me

like a hyena who was about to be eaten by a

bigger, scarier creature for dinner.

ƐAM

CHAPTER 20

It was the scariest thing I'd ever seen. It was terrifying and hairy and it stank. It stank so bad. It was kind of like a man, because it had a head and a body and arms and legs. But it wasn't a man. And it was dirty. So dirty. My brain told me it was a . . .

ZOMBIEEEEEE!

Daniel screamed, too.

We both ran down a long road. I looked over my shoulder. The zombie was still coming, with its arm out, trying to grab us. I ran harder.

When I couldn't see him anymore, I stopped and tried to catch my breath.

Daniel, on the other hand, **threw himself onto the sidewalk** and started wailing like never before.

I wasn't well trained in dealing with crying bullies, or zombies. I took a deep breath and imagined H_2O flying down to help us. Swooping around to keep an eye out in case the zombie turned up again.

And then I sat down next to Daniel on the sidewalk. Even though there was loads of gross dried-up chewing gum on it.

I told him it was going to be OK. When I said that, I felt

like a liar, because I was scared, too, and I didn't really know if it was going to be OK. But that's what grown-ups always say when someone is crying—so I said it.

GROWN-UPS! What would

they do right now?

"Daniel, what would your parents do if they were lost?"

Daniel wiped some snot from his nose with the back of his hand. "They would look for the way on their phones."

"Right. We don't have phones."

"What would yours do? If they were in trouble and were going to die, like us?"

I had to try very hard not to laugh at how dramatic Daniel was being. He actually thought this was the end of the world. Well, the zombie thing was quite scary. But H_2O didn't have to hold back, so I imagined him rolling on the floor laughing instead.

"Well, anytime there's a big problem, my parents always ask Allah. That's one thing they keep telling me a lot, to ask Allah for everything. They say it every day."

Daniel sat up. There was something suddenly different about his face.

I think it was

hope.

"And did you?" he asked.

"Ermm. Actually, no. I forgot," I said sheepishly.

"Ask him!" shouted Daniel. And for a moment, I thought he was going to become the bully Daniel again. But he just sat there waiting, with

BIG, HOPEFUL EYES.

I closed my eyes and whispered a few words, in English. I didn't know the exact Arabic prayer for being lost with a bully and being chased by a zombie, but my dad said that Allah knows all the languages in the universe, so we can talk to him however we need to.

Allah, I'm sorry I forgot to ask you before, but we're kind of lost, and we need your help. We lost all our teachers and we don't know where they are. We don't even know where WE are, actually. And also, there might be a zombie trying to catch us. I'm trying to look after Daniel, but he keeps crying a lot. Please, can you help us? I don't know how, but I guess you know. Thank you. I love you.

I opened my eyes to find Daniel's face right next to mine. "Well? Did you ask him? Is he going to help us?"

"Of course He will. Allah always helps."

"But do you think he heard you? You were whispering so quietly I couldn't even hear you, and I'm right next to you."

"Yes, He did. He's God!" I said in my

WELL, DUHHHH

voice, but then I realized I should be kinder, and explained, "God can hear everything, even whispers, and even what you're saying to yourself in your own head."

"Oh, OK," said Daniel.

Then, because Daniel still looked so frightened and sad, I said, "Don't worry, you'll get back home to your mom and dad, and so will I."

"Yeah, if they even notice I'm gone, or if they even care," said Daniel.

"Of course they care. That's what parents do. Anyway, I think you're a bit hard to miss. I mean, if you weren't there, *I* would notice."

"Really?"

"SUPER DEFINITELY."

Daniel seemed pleased to hear that, for like 0.8 seconds, then his shoulders drooped again.

"Yes, but . . . my parents . . . all they care about is my little sister, Suzy. Because she's always in the hospital."

"Is she . . . is she going to be OK?"

"I don't know, she's always sick and having operations . . ." He started wailing again, as if something was hurting a whole lot. "And I do care about her, I do. I do . . . But what about me?

I might as well not be there. I just get in the way when they need to look after her."

Poor Daniel. **I felt a little lump in my throat**. And I stared at him because I didn't know what to say. So I just moved closer to him, even though he stank of pee, and I said, "I don't know what I would do if that happened to me."

Daniel looked at me as if I had said something that really, really helped. But I had just said the truth, because I didn't know what else to say. He sniffed really hard and wiped his eyes before looking up at me like he was waiting for me to say more.

So I said, "Yeah. You must be **—A REALLY STRONG PERSON.—**

I mean like strong inside, not strong like

BATMAN,

although I think Batman is strong inside as well."

Daniel smiled a snotty smile.

Is this the first time he's ever smiled at me? I thought. That felt really weird. Didn't he hate me?

"So, what now? Do we just sit here?" asked Daniel.

"I don't think so. The **ZOMBIE** might find us."

"What, then?"

"Let's walk."

CHAPTER 21

So we got up and carried on walking the same
way we'd been going before.

Daniel was calmer now. I was kind of proud
of him, and of myself. Even though he did smell
because of the pee in his pants.

After we'd walked for a few minutes, I knew.
I knew why this place was so familiar.

I took Daniel's hand and started running.

And there it was: the huge dome of

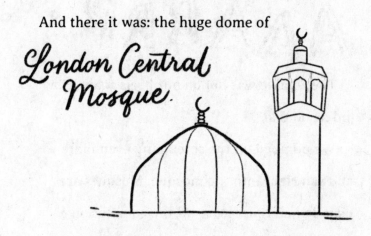

London Central Mosque.

I loved this mosque. This was where I had
had my first halal sweets. This was where
a man had given me money, just for being
cute. This was where I had stood many times,
sometimes with Mom and sometimes with
Dad, and with hundreds of other people, all
praying at the same time. This place was safe.

We ran and ran till we reached the big
space outside the mosque, where I had tried
to ride my scooter once. I looked over my
shoulder, and . . .

AAARRR...

The zombie was hot on our heels again. How did he do that?!

We pumped up the screaming even more and ran right into the mosque. Mosques are usually quiet places, so all the commotion made people come out from all around and come up to us.

There was a man who was wearing one of those Arab-style long things that go right down to the feet. I had one in white. My grandma bought the thobe for me from Mecca. The man had lots of wrinkles and lots of white hair and he was using his hands to signal us

..GGGHHH

to calm down. He was also saying something, but I couldn't hear him, because we were still screaming.

So I stopped.
Then Daniel stopped.

Then I told him everything. It was weird—I felt like I could hear my own voice from far away and it sounded really hysterical. I told him we had gotten lost and tried to find our own way to the Science Museum and then we'd gotten chased by a zombie. Then I realized

iT ALL SOUNDED SUPER CRAZY,

so I quickly told him that we asked Allah for help and ended up here.

The man smiled like he was very proud of us and like he knew all the secrets of the world.

"And where is this zombie, my child?" he asked.

Before I could look around to see where he was, Daniel started pointing and squealing, "There, he's there!"

The man gently took my shoulders and made me look again.

"My dear son," he said. (I wasn't his son, but sometimes people in the mosque who don't know you love you like you're their son.) "That is no zombie. That is a homeless man. And it looks as if he was trying to help you."

I felt like a complete SiLLyHeAd,

because it WAS a homeless man. And he wasn't chasing us. He had just noticed that we were kids, all by ourselves, and he actually cared enough to try to help—but we had run away from him.

I felt pretty bad. I waved at the homeless man sheepishly and he waved back and gave me a yellow-toothed grin. Somebody had sat him down with a cup of tea.

Then the man in the thobe, whose name was Mohamed, sat us down and called our school. A younger man, in jeans and a T-shirt that said

came over and gave us some juice and

halal sweets

This made Daniel's day. (It made mine, too.)

I felt pretty good at this point.

I FELT LIKE
THE HERO
I WAS TRYING
TO BE.

The school had been frantic and had already called the police. Apparently, everyone had been worrying nonstop, especially poor Charlie, and both Daniel's parents and mine had been told.

A policeman and a policewoman showed up about ten minutes later to talk to us. We also got to talk to Eddy, the homeless not-so-zombie man. He was very smiley, even though he doesn't own many clothes or have a house to live in.

"I would've been able to catch up with you if it wasn't for my bad knee!"

He laughed.

As soon as he spoke, I liked him, because he had an accent from up north that sounded just like Reza's. We told him we were sorry for running away from him, and offered him some of our sweets. He liked the red ones the best, just like everyone else I know.

Next, our parents turned up. First mine, and then Daniel's. My mom held on to me and cried and cried, and my dad held on to her.

Everyone decided that it was best that we didn't go to the Wonderlab, as we had had enough adventures for the day. Daniel and I didn't mind. I wondered if he just wanted to stay near his mom, like I did.

Then Dad said, "Come on, Trouble. Let's get you home." And he heaved me onto his shoulder just to make me laugh.

CHAPTER 22

When everything had settled down that evening, Charlie's mom rang my mom and asked if she could bring Charlie over to see me, because

he was a panicky mess

and wanted to make sure I was OK with his own eyes.

So Charlie came over, and we ate cookies with chocolate milk, and I told him all about the zombie thing and about Daniel peeing himself. Then after we finished almost peeing *ourselves* with laughter, I sat up straight and told Charlie that I felt bad for laughing, because **Daniel wasn't too bad at all,** now that I had gotten to know him a bit.

"OK?" said Charlie.

But he didn't seem too sure, so I said, "You'll see. Scout's honor!" and saluted at him. I wasn't a Scout, and Charlie just

again, but I think he believed me.

A couple of days later, my parents invited

Daniel and his family to our house for iftar.

They all wanted to discuss every detail of that

of being lost on the Underground. Mr. and Mrs.

Green seemed nice. I remembered what Daniel had said about feeling like he was just in the way at home. But they were

paying him lots of attention now. His dad

kept ruffling his hair, and his mom kept

touching his shoulder like she wanted to

check he was still there. I had a feeling that

that was why they'd left his sister, Suzy,

with her aunt for this visit—so Daniel could

be their star. They told Mom and Dad that

they were very grateful to the mosque for helping us. Then Daniel told my parents all about how I asked Allah for help and it was only after that that we were saved, so it must have been Allah that did it.

Of course, I had already told them my version of the story, but they were

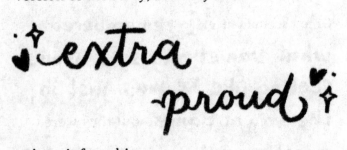

to hear it from him.

Daniel's parents wanted to go to the mosque to thank them again personally, so we had the idea that they should come with us on Eid day and do it then.

Everything was looking really good. I could hardly believe that in just a few days, Daniel

had gone from being the person I liked least
of all to being my friend. He was trying to be
Charlie's friend, too, which was a bit harder
because they're

SOOOOOO  DIFFERENT

from each other.
But I had been an

ACCIDENTAL
MAGNET

again and pulled
them together and
I was completely
super sure they'd
get along. Charlie and I had even asked Daniel

to play soccer with us on the playground, because we realized that nobody had even asked him before. It turned out that he was better than anyone in the whole class at being goalie. But there was still one thing that was bothering me, so I just blurted it out:

"WILL OUR FAMILY BE KICKED OUT OF THE COUNTRY?"

The air in the room suddenly got very thick, like we were on a

with less oxygen or something. Everyone looked very awkward. And since Maryam always giggles in awkward situations, she put her hand over her mouth, but I could still see her shoulders shaking and so could Esa, because he pointed at her with his cheeky grin.

"Where did you get an idea like that?" said Dad.

"ERMMMM." I suddenly realized that I'd gotten it from Daniel, but Daniel would be in trouble if I said anything. I looked at him really quickly and looked away, then I said, "I, erm, heard it somewhere and I even asked Reza, and he said we will have to live in Pakistan."

Dad laughed, but Mom nudged him because she could see that I was serious. Then she smiled politely at the Greens, who looked really

uncomfortable. Daniel was color-matching his

skin with the

on the plate. I wondered if he could feel it when

he went red.

Dad explained that that was never going to

happen, and kids make things up all the time. He

said that I should always talk to an adult to get

the facts right when I hear something like that.

Then Daniel blurted out, **"OK!**
It was me. And
I'm sorry. Omar."

Everyone's heads turned to Daniel really fast. Daniel's head hung toward the floor.

"Well, I heard my cousin Brian saying it, so I just said it to Omar to make him feel bad because I didn't think he'd want to be my friend. But I'm sorry now, anyway."

Mrs. Green's face was doing the color-matching thing with the tomatoes now.

And Mr. Green was saying, "Oh, Daniel." And he was burying his face in his hands.

And then Mrs. Green was saying, "I'm so, so sorry."

And Daniel was saying, "I'm so, so sorry."

And Dad was saying, "Hey, it's okay. Kids will be kids."

And Mom was looking from one person's face to another's.

And then, suddenly, they all went quiet and looked at me.

"Omar, I am very proud that you are Daniel's friend, and I wouldn't want you going anywhere," Mr. Green said.

Phew, I thought.

NOW *everything* IS OK.

I imagined H$_2$O peeking in through the window. He was tiny now, because I didn't need a huge dragon to make me feel better anymore. He winked at me and waved with his tail before flying back off into his cloud.

CHAPTER 23

It was one of the best days of the year—Eid!
And we were going to spend this one with
Mrs. Rogers and the Greens. The night before,
I had stood at my window

TRYING TO SPOT *the* moon,

really, really hoping it would be Eid. The moon
tells us when Ramadan is over, because it's a
new month in the Islamic calendar. If the new

moon can't be seen, it's basically not Eid for another day. When that happens, it's

SO ANNOYING!

The mosque is always very busy on Eid day. Even people who don't normally go to the mosque to pray go on Eid day. So it is absolutely PACKED.

We sat on the carpet, waiting for the prayers to start and watching the people pour in. I like how every single person is different. Different shapes and different sizes, even 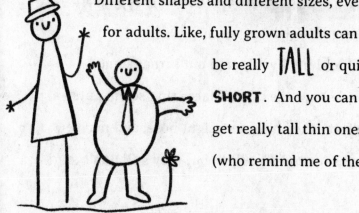 for adults. Like, fully grown adults can be really TALL or quite SHORT. And you can get really tall thin ones (who remind me of the

BFG) and short large ones and all the sizes
in between.

Then (ALL)
the different
types of faces and
shades of colors.

The mosque is great, because you get all types
of people all in one place and you're usually
sitting still for a while, so it's the perfect place
to people-watch.

One thing I've figured out is that some
people have the kind of faces that seem quite
perfect—they have a straight nose, and maybe
good skin and nice lips—but they still don't

look *nice*. Like, I wouldn't want to be stuck in an elevator with them. And they definitely don't smile a lot. Then there are other faces that might have skin that's a bit bad, and maybe their nose isn't the prettiest, or their beard grows in funny directions— but they look really nice! And they SMILE loads. I've thought about it a lot, and I think it's all to do with what's happening *inside people.* If they're always having nice thoughts and are good and kind people, they always look lovely, no matter what. And if they're awful people with rotten thoughts, they'll look horrible. Daniel had been smiling a lot more since we got lost together, and his face was definitely looking much **nicer.**

While the imam led the prayers, the Greens watched from the back. Afterward, they said it was absolutely beautiful, like nothing they'd ever seen before.

Next, we were all going to our home for an

Eid Feast and Presents!

That's the best part of Eid. We had presents for Daniel and his family, too—even Suzy, who had joined us this time.

Daniel rode with me in the Peanut, and on the way he pulled out a little wrapped gift from his jacket pocket and grinned at me.

"It's another Eid present, but for Charlie. It's a Batman key ring . . . Do you think he'll like it?"

"Super definitely." I grinned back.

The feast covered every single centimeter of

our dining table, which we call the Eid Table on Eid. We always put piles and piles of things on the Eid Table because we have lots of friends and family to visit. This year there was:

BIRYANI

SAMOSAS

PAKORAS

ROASTED LEG OF LAMB

and CHICKPEAS IN YOGURT

But what my mouth wanted most of all were the sweet desserts, like the delicious Pakistani thing my mom makes with thin noodles and milk, called SAVAYYAN, and Maryam's special

CHOCOLATE BROWNIES.

Maryam might be super annoying most of the time, but she's getting REALLY good at baking brownies . . .

I sneaked one for myself and one for Daniel before Esa licked them all, like he always does.

"Quick, eat it before anyone else comes in!"

I LAUGHED OUT LOUD.

Daniel gobbled his so fast he got bits of brownie all over his teeth.

"HMNFWHAT?" mumbled Daniel, still with his mouth full.

"Your . . . teeth . . . are . . . so . . . brown!" I snorted.

Daniel started laughing, too. "So are yours!"

TURN THE PAGE FOR A SNEAK PEEK
AT ANOTHER BOOK IN THE

SERIES!

CRR

CHAPTER 1

RASSSHHH!

That was the sound of my ceramic
Stormtrooper bank breaking into 100 pieces.
I had turned it upside down and tapped it
against the metal leg of my desk, because I
thought that was a good idea for getting the
money out. It wasn't. But at least my money
was there, and it looked like **A LOT.**

I needed to get it out to buy this
really cool Nerf laser blaster I saw
on TV. I had accidentally

1

broken my last one the time we had a Nerf

battle at my cousin Reza's house. I'd been

imagining that everyone was turning into

MAN-EATING GIANTS WITH GREEN WARTS ALL OVER THEIR FACES and got a bit

carried away. That's the best part—pretending

you're running from something way scarier

than your cousins and friends.

While I was counting my riches, Maryam

came in and said, "YOU'RE SUCH AN IDIOT. You know there is a little

rubbery piece at the bottom you can just open

the thing with."

"I know," I said. I actually didn't know,

so I felt kind of stupid. I tried really hard to

think of something smart to say, but, in the

meantime, Maryam tried to sit on my wheelie chair, which wheeled itself away from her with a mind of its own. She completely missed the seat and hit the floor, and we both almost wet our pants laughing.

She disappeared back to her room after that, leaving me to add up all my coins and bills. In total, I had $42.53. Super cool—that had to be enough to buy the Nerf blaster! I borrowed

Mom's phone and called my best friend, Charlie.

After I told him, he said,

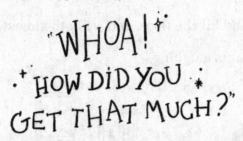

"WHOA! HOW DID YOU GET THAT MUCH?"

"I put all the money I got for Eid and all

the money I got for my birthday in there. Dad

said it would be worth the wait for something

awesome if I saved up."

"Aw, man, that's cool. I spend my money the

minute I get it."

I told Charlie that I used to do that, too, but

then I imagined that if I saved enough money,

one day I could pay people to let me drive even

though I'm only a kid. And maybe I would end

up with enough money to buy a Ferrari, because they're only like $150,000, which surely couldn't take that long to save.

Mom shouted up the stairs that it was time to get off the phone and put my shoes on to go to the mosque. But she said it really nicely and she even called me "sweetie," so I didn't think it was that urgent and I kept talking to Charlie and daydreaming about my Ferrari. Charlie was daydreaming, too, because I said I'd pay people to let him drive as well.

Then Mom came in and blew my ears off.

"I SAID PUT YOUR SHOES ON!"

Yikes!

"Bye, Charlie."

Our mosque trips had become even more fun since Dad started coming with us. He changed things around so that he doesn't have to go to the lab on Saturdays anymore, which means more cool things can happen on weekends now. He even took me go-karting recently, which was the **best Saturday ever!**

Gulp. I couldn't find my left shoe, and Mom was going to lose it if I didn't get this done in fifteen milliseconds . . . Yes! I saw it

on top of the sofa and grabbed it while Dad

stood over me with a face like that emoji

whose lips are just a very straight line. But

when I went to put it on, I saw that it had

been treated to a dose of my little brother's

slime in a bucket.

I didn't dare complain

or look for other shoes,

so I shoved my foot in. It

was DISGUSTING. Like I

was stepping on a

GAZILLION
ZOMBIE
EYEBALLS.

Ewwwwwwww.

I squished and SQUIRTED my way to the
Peanut (that's our car) and jumped in.

At the mosque, when we were all praying,
Esa sat on my head and made me laugh. I
had to control myself before it turned into a
full-on giggle fit, so I imagined that there was
a SUPER-VILLAIN holding me in a
headlock and if I laughed out loud, he would
blow up the whole entire universe. But if I
kept quiet as a mouse, he would release me
and the universe would be safe . . .

PHEW. I managed it. I was pretty
pleased with myself, especially when Dad
turned and winked at me when the prayer
was finished. I know why he did it. To show
me that he saw Esa on my head and that he

was proud of how I'd handled it. Also because he was in a good mood. He's always in a good mood at the mosque, and he has a different sort of smile on his face while we're there. Maybe it's a *secret smile* that's only for Allah or something. I think he's really glad we found such a great mosque close to our new house. All the others Mom made us try out when we first moved are miles away. Dad says he's happy that it has the kind of vibes that make him feel closer to Allah. Mom and Dad like those kinds of vibes, and they say you don't get them in every mosque. Everyone is really nice to each other, and it's quiet, and light comes streaming in through the windows on sunshiny days.

CHAPTER 2

On Monday at school, I rolled in with an imaginary Nerf blaster in my arms and targeted my best friend, Charlie.

He gave me the very same toothy grin that made me like him when I moved to this school recently. Then he pulled out his own blaster from under the table (imaginary, too, of course) and pretended to blast me right back.

I think his imagination has been getting

stronger since we became friends, like a muscle

does when you lift weights all day long.

When Daniel saw us, he giggled and punched

me on the arm. Don't worry, it was

one of those friendly punches that

don't hurt at all. Daniel is our friend now. He

doesn't actually bully anyone anymore, not even Charlie, who used to be his favorite target for all things horrible. There's no way we'd be friends with a bully, but it turns out Daniel had reasons for being so naughty at school, and now that he has us as friends to hang out with, he's

TOTALLY DIFFERENT.

"It's a Nerf laser blaster," I announced. "Imaginary for now, but I'm going to get a real one with the money I've saved."

"Oh, cool!" said Daniel. "I want one."

"Me too!" chipped in Charlie.

"Let's all get them and have an

EPIC NERF BATTLE."

"We can all pretend to be spies, like James Bond chasing down an evil villain," Daniel said excitedly.

OH YEAAAAH!

Charlie and I said at the same time. We often say things at the same time, which is super funny and sometimes super freaky.

"Do you have enough money?" I asked.

"No, but my mom said she was going to

buy me something for, ummmm . . ." Daniel
sheepishly scratched the back of his head
instead of finishing his sentence.

"For what?"

Charlie and I did it AGAIN. Same words,
same time. Same wanting to know what Daniel
was getting a treat for.

"Umm . . ."

"For washing your dad's car?" I guessed.

"For cleaning your room?" Charlie guessed.

Daniel did some more sheepish head-
scratching.

I tried another guess. "For getting ten out of
ten on your spelling test?"

"No . . . no . . . um . . . actually for
'settling in so much better at school and
making such good friends,'" Daniel said,

using air quotes as he blushed bright red.

Charlie and I both jumped onto Daniel to give him a **hug**. I think he was blushing because he's not always 100% sure that we like him as our friend, but we super definitely do. We keep finding so many things that we like to do together—like the Nerf blasters!

We couldn't help but talk about it all during math, because it was way more exciting than learning about what a denominator was and how we could think about a pizza in fractions. The only thing I think when I see a pizza is how quick I can get it into my mouth. Mrs. Hutchinson was very excited about fractions. I could tell because her curly hair was all big and springy. That's one thing I like about Mrs. Hutchinson—she thinks everything is entertaining.

"I CANNOT WAIT for the Nerf battle. It's going to be crazy fun!" I whispered.

Charlie whispered back, "I knooowww. I just have to think of a way to convince my parents to buy me a blaster, too."

"You do know that both of you whisper as loud as you talk," Daniel pointed out.

He must have been right, because Mrs. Hutchinson came over, attempting to put her cross face on, and said, "Stop chatting and tell me how much pizza is on the board, boys."

"Not enough for me," said Daniel.

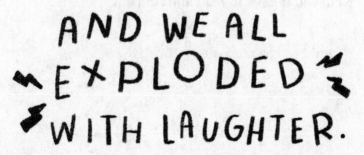

AND WE ALL EXPLODED WITH LAUGHTER.

When Omar's favorite teacher goes missing, it's up to him and his friends to save her from . . . well, you'll have to read and find out!

Omar is a hero for taking the blame when his friend gets in trouble at school, but when something more serious happens, will everyone believe that it wasn't him?

DID YOU KNOW YOU CAN LISTEN TO ALL OF OMAR'S STORIES, TOO?

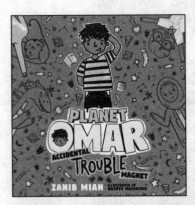

Audiobooks available to download now!